Good day, mate!
I am so glad you could come and join us.
I am Mr. Wilson the Worm,
and I am here with my new friend, Tommy.
I am from the down-under city of
Wagga Wagga, Australia.
I want to tell you a story about all the work we worms do.
Look for "Fun Facts" about worms
at the bottom of each page!

FUN FACT:
Worms do not have eyes.
Baby worms hatch from a cocoon
and are the size of a grain of rice when they hatch.

My friend Tommy has a problem.
He wants to plant a garden filled with tomato plants,
but this patch of ground is way too hard.
Tommy is in luck.
My crew and I are here to help him.

FUN FACT:
Worms help soil get the air and water plants need.
Without air and water, the soil would be too hard for plants to grow.

Here is my crew:
Lou, Ed, Gabi, and Sid.
We are at your service,
willing and able to help.

FUN FACT:
Worms have simple brains, but they have five hearts.

Worms are earth's construction workers.
We love to dig in dirt.
That's what we were created to do.

FUN FACT:
Worms eat dirt to clean the soil.
They are natural recycling plants!

My crew and I will dig tunnels in this hard patch of dirt.
This way, water and air can move freely through the dirt,
making it healthy soil.
Our digging will help get the soil ready
for Tommy to plant his tomato plants in the garden.

FUN FACT:
Worms break up the soil
by making tunnels so air and water
can circulate through the soil.

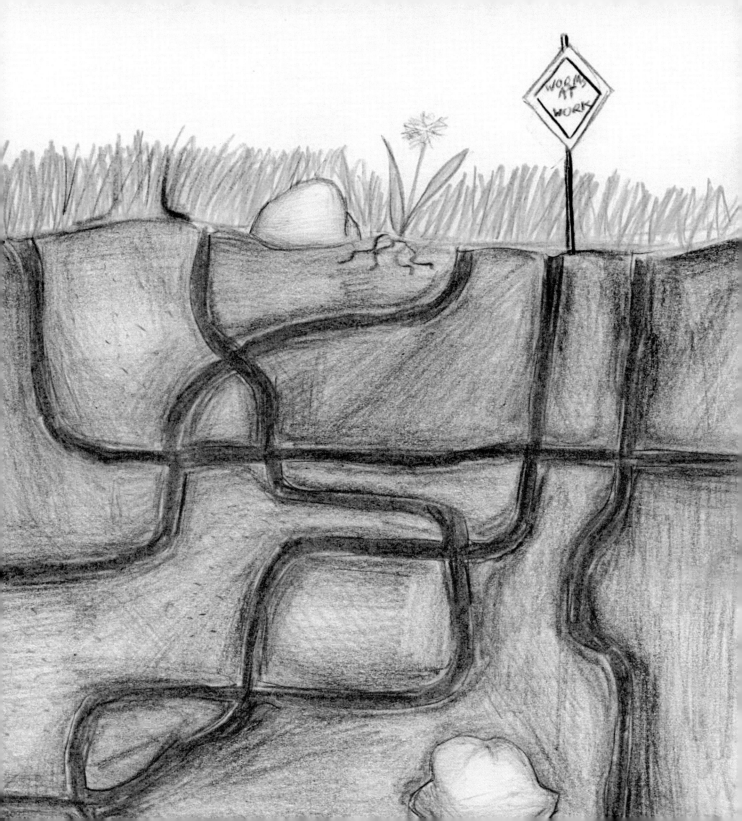

OK, crew, a few things to remember:
Stay away from birds
and people who like to use us as bait to catch fish!

FUN FACT:
Worms serve as food for other animals.
Worms can lose parts of their bodies,
but they will grow back.

13

I told my crew not to eat anything but dirt.
Every once in a while my crew can get tempted by something else—
like Tommy's apple over there.
They just might help themselves to a bite.
Hey, Lou! Hey, Gabi!
Get out of that apple
and get back to work!

(NOT SO) FUN FACT
Some people eat worms as part of their food source.

That was a good day's work.
Job well done!
Now let's do a worm dance
to help bring on the rain.

FUN FACT:
Worms must stay moist, or they will die.
They do not have noses. They breathe through their skin.

I feel the wind starting to blow.

I see the rain clouds coming our way.

Yes! It is starting to rain.

Our soil needs rain.

FUN FACT:
Worms do not have bones in their bodies.

Thank you, Lou, Ed, Gabi, and Sid.
Good job! Well done!
Take a bow for all your hard work.
Clap for them, everyone!

GOOD ADVICE:
Whatever you do, work at it with all your heart.
Colossians 3:23

Tommy worked hard digging
and planting his tomato plants.
All his hard work has paid off.
Tommy has a beautiful garden
filled with tomatoes.

FUN FACT:
Worms have light sensitive cells,
so they can tell if it is day or night..
They are scattered throughout their skin.

Well, it is good-bye for now, mates.
I hope you had fun! I know I did.
Thank you for letting me share my world with you.
If you ever need help with a garden,
remember me, Mr. Wilson the Worm, and my crew
from the down-under city of
Wagga Wagga, Australia.

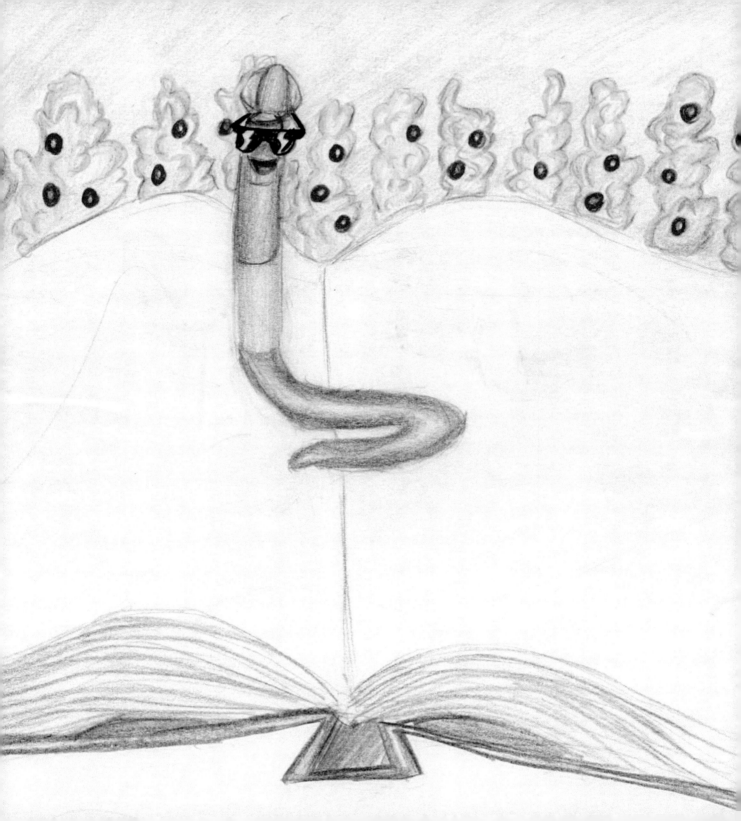